Something in the Sky

SOMETHING IN THE
SKY

FIRST BOOK IN THE LYLE KENT SERIES

JUNE A. REYNOLDS

ILLUSTRATIONS BY:

CLYDE LIST AND
CRYSTAL ANZALDI

ReadersMagnet, LLC

TABLE OF CONTENTS

Introduction: Something in the Sky

He sat on the broken rubble of rock and stared out into the setting sun. There was something in the sky or maybe it was something in the air that was trying to communicate with him. You could see forever out here in the desert. That butte over there looked maybe a mile away, but on the map it was twenty miles. Even the stillness in the air was talking to him, and Lyle felt like this spot was where he wanted to stay forever. Blue sky was turning to purple and pink in every direction. He loved his life, although he was always a little nervous in the back of his head because of his father in Afghanistan.

The sun caught some high horsetail clouds floating off to the east and cast them in hot pink. Horsetail clouds meant a change in the weather. In Arizona it was not very common to have change. Every day seemed the same. The sunglow on the horizon hovered over the desert, hinting at more of a day, but it was a false promise, followed by an ever deepening of the dark.

Lyle jumped up from his perch and walked home in the dark. The light-colored rocks lining the trail guided his way off the hill and down into the subdivision lighted by high streetlamps.

In His Own Words: Lyle Kent

All the lights were on in my house. That seemed pretty unusual. Mom never kept any lights on unless there was someone in the room. That was the rule at our house: "Turn off the light when you leave the room." The place looked like a pyramid with a wide line of lights on the first floor, then less and less to the top. There was one light on in the attic! Oh cripes! Did Teddy lock himself in the bathroom again? Or maybe he decided to play hide-and-seek by himself. Or maybe Baby Mary fell off the bed? He always felt guilty when things like that happened, but it was impossible for him to be around every minute of the day to help. It was driving him crazy.

Unfortunately, things seemed to be even worse than that. There was a cop at the front door and several expensive-looking cars parked all over the place. A couple of neighbors were already on the scene, whispering to each other.

"Uh, hi," I said to the cop. "Um, I'm Lyle and I live here."

"Really?" The cop's eyes bugged out. "Well, just a minute." He talked into his walkie-talkie on his shoulder. "There's a kid out here named Lyle. He says he lives in this house. Should I let him in?"

There was dead air, then an electronic crackle. "Roger that. Let him in."

So there I was, entering my house, awaiting certain doom.

Losing It

There was quite a crowd of people in the living room. Almost as many as there was the last time Dad left for Afghanistan. My mom was sitting in the middle of the couch bent over, weeping and sobbing. Baby Mary was sitting on the floor watching Mom with wide eyes, and four-year-old Teddy was sitting next to Mom not knowing what to do.

"Mom, what is going on?" I rushed over and sat down next to her and held her clammy hand. Everyone else in the room just watched uncomfortably.

"Oh, Lyle, we've lost the house! It's being repossessed!"

"Mom, how did that happen?" We had lived there for five years, and we never had any problems before.

"Well, remember when your dad and I got a second mortgage on the house?" She was looking at me expectantly, like I knew what she was talking about.

"No, Mom. I'm a kid. I don't know what you're talking about."

"Well, we got some money from the value of the house to hold us over until your father got his first paycheck, but I guess your dad didn't pay the mortgage for a few months." She shuddered. "Now we have to move out of the house."

"How could this happen, Mom? That would be gobs of money, wouldn't it? I mean, where is all that money now? I mean, did we really need that much money?" I was just grasping at straws without a clue.

Mom was sobbing. "I don't know about any of this, Lyle. I let your dad handle all the money. I haven't heard from him in over a week."

I grabbed Mom's shoulders and looked her in the face. "Mom! What are we going to do? Can't we get some money together or go stay with Aunt Peggy?"

Someone cleared their throat. "Uh, Ms. Kent, considering that you have your hands full and all, I'll give you a week from today to make arrangements and get out of here. Let's go, everyone, and let these people get their life together." Suddenly everyone was gone except for me, Teddy, Mary, and Mom. Teddy, who had been silent the whole time, started wailing.

Things started happening fast after that. Mom started hauling everything out in the front yard and began a perpetual garage sale. We used the computer to put all the big things like the washer, dryer, refrigerator, and freezer on Craigslist. Mom had to let our once-a-week housekeeper go. She bought most of Baby Mary's stuff because she was going to have a baby.

I guess that this economy was pretty bad already because we could not stay with Aunt Peggy. She had her daughter home from college, and her son and his family lived in their travel trailer. At first, I thought we were just going to move somewhere else in town, but the rents were high, Mom could not find a job, and we just did not have enough money. Mom tried to contact Dad through email, phone, and Skype. He was not at the base camp, so we thought he was on patrol somewhere in the mountains.

With two days to go, before the bank was going to kick us out, my mom made an announcement at breakfast: "Well, everyone, I have some exciting news. We are going on an adventure!"

"Yay!" yelled Teddy.

I was not so fast to be excited. "Uh, Mom, what exactly do you mean?"

"We are going on an exciting trip to Oregon to stay with your great-grandpa!"

"Mom," I protested, "I just started high school! You want me to go to another high school?"

Mom's face darkened. "No, of course I don't want you to go to another high school. I don't want any of this, Lyle, but I have no choice. When my mom and dad died in a car crash, I didn't have any choice, and we don't have any choices now, except this. You will get to go to the same high school that I went to when I was your age. I stayed at Grandpa's place, and Aunt Peggy was put in foster care for a year before she graduated."

I tried to recall who this person was that we were going to live with. "When was the last time you saw your grandpa, Mom?"

"When I was eighteen," she said grimly.

The Bad News

I was sort of a borderline popular kid at school. Oh, okay, I admit, I was really more on the fringes of popularity. My problem is that I am a small person, and I look young for my age. I have golden curly hair that has a mind of its own, so with those looks, no one takes me seriously. I had a friend (not girlfriend) in the next cul-de-sac named Kate, and she had three very popular brothers who were football and basketball stars. Kate and I had just started high school, and so we were thrilled with the prospect of being high-rolling freshmen on campus. But then this stupid house thing had to happen.

I caught up with Kate on the sidewalk as everyone was walking to the bus stop. "Kate, Kate, slow down! I've got to talk to you."

She laughed and started running. She called back, "You've got to get into training, Lyle, if you are going to be in the homecoming relay. Come on!"

I stopped in my tracks. "I'm not going to be here for Homecoming." As I said that, I choked back my tears. I couldn't have her brothers see me like that.

Kate slowed down and turned around. "What? You've got to be kidding me."

"I am not kidding you, Kate." I gulped back my tears. The look on my face made her walk back.

"So where are you going? Will you be back for Halloween?" she asked.

"It looks like I won't be coming back here at all. My mom and dad lost our house, and the only place we can go until Dad gets back is Oregon."

Kate stamped her foot. "Oh, Lyle! That is horrible! I was going to have you be my escort if I got homecoming princess!"

On the Road

Each of us packed a rolling luggage bag of belongings. We stored photo books and keepsakes at Aunt Peggy's. When the car sold, Mom didn't think we should buy airplane tickets, so we went on the train instead. It was a good thing that she squirreled away all the money she could.

A week from the day that all the people came, we said goodbye to our beautiful house. Mom laid the front-door and backdoor keys on the kitchen counter and said, "Goodbye, house, I thought that I was going to live here forever." And she walked out with Baby Mary. Teddy followed behind.

"Be there in a minute, Mom," I called. I felt that there was something I could not leave behind. I looked at the keys lying there and felt a twinge of revenge in my heart. I ran back up to my room and found an old pair of shoes and took out the shoelace. I went back down and put the keys on the lace and put it around my neck. I put it down my shirt so my mom would not see them. I really didn't know why I did that, but it seemed the right thing to do at the time. I felt like if I was not going to be allowed to live in this house, no one else should either.

Aunt Peggy was out front stuffing the bags and kids in the car. We sped off to the train station, and we hardly had time to get there. We had to quickly say goodbye and get on the train. I was in charge of the laptop, my bag, and Teddy and his bag. It was exciting to leave on the train and get used to the constant movement. Soon the desert countryside started to look all alike and the excitement wore off.

"Are we there yet?" asked Teddy.

"No, but almost," said Mom, as she winked at me. For five days we stayed on the train. Mom only got one sleeper bunk, and it was really little so I would sit up at night in the seat. Mom traded off with me a couple of times, and I tried to sleep with the kids, but that was worse than sleeping in the seats. The days wore on, and I was glad that I'd packed comic books and a few reading books to pass the time and distract Teddy. We had to get off the train one time in Sacramento and spend the night in the train station. It was really creepy hanging out with all the people. That was really a night of no sleep.

A New State

Finally, we made it to Oregon. There were many different kinds of trees and all kinds of mountains and rivers. It was raining the minute we got in the mountains, and it never stopped until we got to Portland. There was so much more to see, and Teddy was mesmerized. "Oh, man! It is so green!" he said. He was right. I had never seen so many shades of green in my life.

We came around the bend of a mountain, and there, way below was a river with huge rapids foaming and splashing all the way across the river!

Mom pointed to the riverside of the train. "Wow! Look, kids! The Willamette River is really flooding! There's a whole tree over there floating in the water."

Mom and everyone in our car had their heads up to the glass. The river was full of foam, and the wind carried some of it right up to the window. There were six waterfalls feeding into the frothing river.

We followed the river to a calm, flat area with more railroad tracks, and we watched trains coming and going around us. Soon we had cars on either side of us. On one side, the cars were not moving, but we were moving one way and another train was moving rapidly the other way. It was like being in a deep canyon with moving sides. Teddy threw up.

Finally, we were in a busy city. We crossed a tall bridge and slowly came down near a huge brick station with a clock tower and a sign that said Go by Train. It was Union Station, and we were in downtown Portland.

"Are you folks going to be picked up?" asked the porter. "I could stack up your stuff over on the loading dock."

"Thanks," said Mom, "but we need to get on bus 12."

"No bus 12 anymore," said the porter. "You need to get on the light-rail to Pioneer Courthouse Square, then you will get on the 94, on Broadway, to go any farther. At the transit station in Tigard, you get on the 12. Sherwood is at the end of the line."

Mom started to make some phone calls, but didn't seem to get an answer. We all just collapsed around our bags and waited. Finally, Mom said, "Let's go." And we all got up and straggled down the sidewalk toward the light-rail stop. The electric cars were fun, but it didn't go very far before we had to get off and wait for the bus. The first bus was crowded until we got to Tigard. We got off the bus and were told to run to the bus in front of it. It was a huge struggle to drag our stuff and Teddy and Mary off the bus. Teddy fell down on the sidewalk, and I stopped to pick up him and his rolling bag. Mom was racing to the bus, just as the door slammed shut and started to drive away. I just about collapsed to the ground, when bus 94 let off the loudest and longest honk I've ever heard. The 12 bus screeched to a stop, and the driver actually got off. The driver of the 94 also got off the bus.

Driver 94 yelled, "What is wrong with you? This is the third time I've seen you do this! Can't you wait a few minutes for these poor people?"

"I didn't see anyone get off your bus!" Driver 12 retorted as he stomped back to his bus. We had no choice but to follow him, but Driver 94 grabbed Teddy's rolling suitcase and walked him to the bus.

"Let's see if we can get this right!" Driver 94 shouted into the bus.

Driver 12 slapped the door shut in his face.

The bus was crowded, but by the time we got to Sherwood, we were the only ones on the bus. Mom was calling and calling on her cell and not getting an answer from Grandpa. I started getting that worried feeling in the back of my head, just like I get about Dad.

Walking to Middleton

"Well, I think we should start walking," said Mom. It was late in the afternoon on a partially cloudy day. I kept thinking it was going to rain at any moment, like it does in Arizona when we see some clouds. It was the first of November, and the leaves from the trees were now like old muddy snowdrifts. Teddy was kicking at a pile of mucky leaves, and I stopped him because he was getting his shoes wet and dirty.

We started down a graveled trail that connected to the railroad tracks, crossed them, and got onto a sidewalk. I'm sure we looked like quite a parade with Mom leading the way with a baby backpack, purse, and diaper bag strung like bandoleers, pulling a rolling suitcase. Next came Teddy with his rolling suitcase, tipping over every three minutes, and me in the rear with a flight bag, laptop case, and another rolling suitcase. Some people honked at us, and someone yelled out the window, "Pioneer Days!" (Whatever that meant.)

The hill got steeper, and our parade was strung out along ways over three blocks. Teddy's rolling suitcase had not only tipped over but also was spilling out on the sidewalk. I stopped to stuff his clothes back in and saw Mom at the top of the hill.

I called, "Mom, Mom, we will never make it. I'm going to see if we can hitchhike." She waved at me, but I don't think she really heard me.

I stuck out my thumb and tried to smile as a yellow SUV roared by. "Get a job!" yelled a boy out the window.

"Teddy," I commanded. "Stay right there. We are going to get a ride."

"But I can't see, Mommy!" he wailed.

I stuck out my thumb and a couple more cars passed us up. It was getting darker. Suddenly, a big black GMC van/truck thing pulled up. The hulk was pretty battered up, and a big lady got out.

"Hi there, kid. I'm Madge Brookman. You look like you've got your hands full."

"Hi, Ms. Brookman. Could you give us a ride to Middleton? My mom and sister are at the top of the hill," I said. "Oh, my gosh, yeah!" she exploded. She quickly opened the back door, scooped up Teddy, and grabbed his bag all in one fell swoop. She seated Teddy between two baby seats. "These are the twins, Billy and Milly. What's his name?"

"That's Teddy and I'm Lyle," I said as I piled everything in the back of the GMC.

We took off up the hill, but didn't see Mom until we got to the intersection. Mom was sitting at the stop sign with all of her stuff piled around her and Baby Mary in her arms, crying hysterically. I got out of the van and quieted her down. Then with Ms. Brookman's swift and efficient help, we got loaded up.

"Where to? asked Madge.

"Pigeage," said Mom weakly.

Madge exclaimed, "Oh, *man*! I haven't heard that name for a long, long time. You know old man Lowe?" "Yes, he's my grandfather," said Mom.

We turned up Middleton Road. Mom was looking around, but I could tell that she didn't recognize the place. Finally, we came to a dark driveway, and Madge turned down the dirt road. We passed huge dark piles that looked partly like buildings, and there at the end of the drive was a wrecked car and a large, wide house with a big porch. There were no lights anywhere, so Madge kept on the headlights while Mom went up to the porch to knock on the door. No one answered, so she came back.

"I think there is someone in there. I could hear a TV or radio. He knows I'm coming, but maybe he can't hear because of the program," said Mom.

"He's pretty feeble these days," mused Madge. "Maybe you and I should just go in, if he's expecting you."

"I'm going too," I blurted.

"Me too," said Teddy.

So after a bit of squabbling, we all went in. First we unloaded the suitcases on the porch, hoping that the old man would come out, but that didn't do any good. So we knocked again and since no one came to the door, we walked in. We called, "Oh, Mr. Lowe! Grandpa! We're here!" No response. Madge lead the way with her emergency flashlight as we threaded through piles of boxes and newspapers. There was dust on the floor and creepy cobwebs everywhere.

"I'm scared," whispered Teddy. I flipped on a light at the stairway and told Teddy to stay there.

We went into the living room that was lit by one lamp, and there was an old man sitting in a chair in front of a blaring TV. His eyes were open, but he was breathing like he was asleep.

"Grandpa, Grandpa, it's Gail. I'm here. Wake up, Grandpa!" said Mom.

Grandpa blinked his eyes and stared blankly at Mom. I could not believe this was happening. Grandpa looked like he was going to die. We had come so far to survive, and we came to this?

Grandpa opened his dry mouth. "Are you from a tribe or a kingdom?"

"It's Gail, Grandpa. I'm from a tribe."

Grandpa's face broke into a wonderful smile, and I knew, with relief, that we were going to stay.

Getting Settled In

The next week was a blur for me. Madge told me where to catch the bus, and I went to the high school. It was not the same building that Mom went to. They changed that into a junior high. I went to the office and the counseling center. They gave me classes that I thought were for the sophomore grade, but they told me that these classes were for freshmen. Who was I to argue with the experts?

I went around to all the classes, and I'll have to say I would hear about six sentences the teacher would say and the rest sounded like *blah blah blah.*

I got home at night on the bus, and there would be an endless list of chores to do: take out the garbage, sweep the floors, vacuum the living room, watch the baby, wash the dishes. For a person who had a spotless three-story home and a once-a-week maid, my mom rose to the occasion at Grandpa's house and managed to chip away all the grime from the toilet and sinks and wash all the towels and bedding in the whole house. She washed and cleaned all the windows and curtains. Madge got a Lions Club member to come and haul away all the newspapers. That gave us a lot more room, and Grandpa didn't seem to miss them at all.

Firemen's Chicken

The next week, on Monday, I came home to a silent house. The hair on the back of my head started to move at the unusual nonsound. I put my coat and hat on a hook, then I heard Baby Mary shrieking in the kitchen. I ran to the disaster scene, only to find everyone sitting around the big round table with a huge platter in the center heaped with what looked like leftover chicken, covered with goo.

Teddy sat there in a trance, eyes wide, breathing in the warm barbecue perfume.

"Look, Lyle!" said Mom. "Meals on Wheels brought us chicken and baked potatoes!"

"Wow," I said sarcastically. "Isn't Meals on Wheels only supposed to feed old people? Aren't they breaking the law or something?"

"Let's quit stallin' and put on the feed bag!" yelled Grandpa.

"We need to use our quiet voice," said Morn to Grandpa. "Please help yourself."

Mom didn't seem concerned about the origin of the chicken as she dished up a gooey chicken leg to Teddy. "I think there is no need to worry about the chicken, Lyle. The wife of the chief of police brought the food herself, so it must be okay."

"It could be entrapment," I mused, remembering a recent civics lesson.

"What's this black stuff?" screeched Teddy as he lifted a sheet of goo hanging to his chicken leg. It dropped onto the table, and he picked up the goo with his fingers and dangled it in the air.

"That's barbecue chicken skin," said Mom calmly

"Ewwww!" shrieked Teddy.

Grandpa, who had been concentrating on his food, startled at the shriek. "Wal, stick it to the top of your plate, boy, and eat the rest, for cripes sakes." Grandpa actually had practical suggestions at times.

As Mom served up a breast of chicken to herself, she said grandly, "This is not just any chicken, Lyle, but is the fabulous barbecued Fireman's Chicken, made right here in Sherwood."

"Really?" said Teddy as he picked up the chicken leg and took too big of a bite.

"Mom," I said, "I don't think we should take all this fantastic chicken from the poor old people. I think we should get on food stamps, and I could get free lunch and breakfast at school."

"Excellent idea, son," quipped Grandpa. "We should all do our part for the war effort. Gail, I'll watch the kids. You go downtown tomorrow and get our war ration coupons."

"Yes, Dad," said Mom, ignoring the time warp.

I grabbed a plate and took two thighs and the biggest baked potato. They were only lukewarm, but really good. "It's not bad," I concluded, "but why doesn't Meals on Wheels ever serve anything good like pizza or tacos?"

"They want us to be healthy," said Mom, "so you all can grow big and strong."

"I'm gonna be a big fireman and cook barbecued chicken!" proclaimed Teddy.

Yeah, I thought, *all firemen do every day is torch barbecued chicken.* I didn't say it out loud, though. I don't really like to discourage Teddy.

Meeting Benny

After two weeks of school, I felt like I was getting into the swing of things. Getting the free lunch was easy with some paperwork from the school office. On the first morning of my free food, I got in the breakfast line with my card and was surprised by someone tapping my shoulder.

"Hi! I'm Benny," said this cute little guy who looked like a pixie.

"Uh, hi. I'm Lyle. Do you go to school here?"

"Yeah, uh, no. Uh, yes...sorta...I'm in eighth grade, but I work here in special ed for two periods a day. Are you in eighth grade too?" he asked.

I was a really small kid, and I was probably the youngest kid in my class because my birthday is in December, so I got questions like that all the time. "I'm a freshman."

"I see you on the bus. You live out on Middleton Road. I work with my cousin. He is a freshman too and is in special ed."

"Oh, I see," I said, not really understanding.

We scanned our card and got a tray of food. Benny was waiting for something. You could see it in his eyes. He was about to explode as we hit the table.

"Can I tell you something very embarrassing?" he whispered.

"No, Benny, you cannot," I said. I know how these little kids work.

We wolfed down our tray load of food, the bell rang, and we were off to class.

The next day, Benny was after me again. "I've got a problem, Lyle, and I need some help."

I could tell that he was very serious and not at all being jokey, so I thought I'd give him a listen. "Okay, Benny, I will help you as long as you aren't trying to joke me."

"Okay." he exhaled with relief. "My cousin, Wade, in special ed? I work with him you know."

"Yeah, that's what you said."

"Well, this adult aide, Ms. Betts, told me that I have to change his diaper! I don't know how to change a diaper!" His eyes filled with tears.

I could tell that Benny was really upset about this, so I took a stand. "I think the adult should change the diaper."

"Well, me too, Lyle, that's what they did when Wade was at the middle school, but she is not going to do it. She says I have to do it. What am I going to do? I may lose my job." Benny started scratching his arms.

"Calm down, Benny, you don't get paid to do this job, so don't do it!" I exclaimed.

"It's not that easy, Lyle. This is my cousin we're talking about. I can't leave him in this mess," said Benny in tears.

"Literally," I mumbled.

So we finished our food and went to the special ed room. I explained to Benny that I was an expert diaper changer with two babies under my belt. He was so relieved to have his problem solved, but I explained to him we were not out of the woods yet. He would have to watch, learn, and practice; you don't just start diapering like a champ on the first try.

Wade was off the special ed bus and was cruising around the room looking at the decorations for fall on the bulletin boards and drawing with his fingers on all the computer screens. A lady was working on a clipboard, and as soon as she looked up, she said, "Benny, change Wade. He's already wet. Who's that?"

Benny just stood there.

"I'm Benny's friend. I was just going." Benny gripped my hand.

"Good," she said, without looking at us, as she stepped into an office.

We rounded up Wade and took him into the changing area. "Undo his pants, Benny," I instructed.

"Uh, okay, but I've never–"

"Look, Benny," I said, "we are helping your cousin. He is helpless, and it is your duty to help him. That is all there is to this."

"You are right, Lyle." As soon as Benny opened Wade's trousers, the kid pulled them down all by himself and lay down on his own.

This was too good to be true. "Oh my gosh, Benny, this is too easy! Wade knows what you are doing. He's done this a million times," I said as the first period bell rang. I held up a large disposable diaper. "Now you see these two tabs? Open them and take the front part down. Now lift his fanny, and slide the old diaper out. Maybe lift the legs a bit? Fold it fast and try to re-stick the diaper so you don't get any pee or poo all over the place."

As I did all this, Wade actually lifted his hips ever so slightly and the diaper was off and wrapped up.

"Now clean him off with these wipes. Yeah, good, no matter what it is, always clean your subject. Use a lot of them if you don't have to pay for them. Yeah, good work, Benny."

I held up the new diaper. "Now look at this new diaper. See this bunched up part? That is the back. Unfold the diaper and put the back part under Wade. Lift his leg a bit, yeah, there see, he knows you want to put it under him. Now spread the front and check around his legs so it looks a bit sealed. Now pull the tabs in back, one at a time and stick them on the front, but not too tight, adjust that, Benny! You don't want to cut him in half!"

We pulled Wade up and pulled his pants back on.

We took him to the sink, and we all washed our hands.

Wade was really excited about this and got some water on his shirt. Benny was beaming. "Thank you, Lyle! I think I can do this! I love you. You are my best friend." He gave me a great big hug just as the adult aide, Ms. Betts, walked into the bathroom.

"Why are you still here? The bell rang fifteen minutes ago. Get to class!" she spat.

I grabbed my stuff and bolted out the door. The hall was quiet as I walked to my class, but when I got there, the door to the room was locked. Mr. Hill, the civics teacher, warned us that if we were late, he would lock the door and we would be marked absent. There would already be a phone call at the house that would say I was skipping.

Walking the Vineyard

Starting that next Saturday morning, my new chore was to take Grandpa out of the house so Mom could clean the living room. With Baby Mary aka the rug rat in the house, we had to vacuum the floor once a week, and it was hard to do with an old man smack dab in the middle of it.

We started our first outdoor ramble by walking all over the old winery. Grandpa had started the winery in the early 1960s, just before my mom came to live with him the first time. He started by actually growing all of the plants in greenhouses. The broken, old greenhouses were all over the place.

Grandpa's estate, "Pigeage," was at one time filled with practical barns and outbuildings, which were now punctured by towering blackberry bushes and deflated by the weight of snow drifts from decades of harsh winters.

"What does Pigeage mean, Grandpa?" I asked. "Well, 'Pigeage' is a step in making wine, especially the Pinot Noir wine, where the skins of the grapes want to float on top. It's not good with them on top. You can't get a good chemical reaction, you know, so you do a Pigeage by pressing down the skins and seeds that float to the top of the vat. You've got to get those juices flowing," he said with a smile.

"How did you learn all this stuff, Grandpa?" I asked.

"By doing a lot of listening–I mean really listening to what people say. By listening to the old farmers around here you could learn as much as you could learn in any biology or home ec class at high school. I learnt all this wine making from the Italian Cerenghinos–the onion farmers down there in Cipole."

We walked down to the grape field itself and looked at the scraggly vines already tom up by with fall rains. The grass in the field was flattened now, but you could tell that it had not been tilled like most vineyards I had seen. Then I remembered why. His tractor was buried alive in one of the old busted up buildings and Grandpa couldn't get it out.

"What are these weird red bark trees out here, Grandpa? I asked.

"They are madrones. Seedlings brought in by birds. Look at their flaking skin, just like a snake in the summer."

Then Grandpa did a weird thing. He threw his arms into the air and talked to the trees in a poem:

Open your flaking, rusty limbs to the sky,

My little Madrones.

Reach into the blue sky

To catch the birds.

I smiled. "That's cool, Grandpa. Did you make that up or are they song lyrics?"

Grandpa chuckled. "It's the song of nature, son, it's in the air all around us, if we stop to listen."

*****

To: Dan.Kent@us.army.mil

From: *LKent@sherwoodsd.kl2.or.us*

Hi Dad,

I bet you have a huge list of emails right now from Mom, but I thought I would let you know what we are doing. We lost the house in Arizona, and we sold everything so that we could go to Oregon to live with Mom's grandpa. He actually has an old winery, but I suppose you already knew that. He is not always in good shape. He looks like he is asleep most of the time. Mom is doing a great job fixing up the house. We could really use a car, so if you get any money please send it. Mom wastes a lot of time riding the bus. Sometimes she gets Madge to drive her to the bus stop, but not always. She has to take both Mary and Teddy with her because she can't trust Grandpa to babysit, so it is not easy to get around. We have food stamps now, so we get pizza once a week. I am going to Sherwood High School—the same school Mom went to when she was a kid, except it is a different, newish building. I am staying after school a couple of days a week now to catch up on my schoolwork, so I have time to write on the school computers! Sweet! Bye for now.

Love Lyle.

*****

Mom was not so excited about me staying after school on Tuesdays and Wednesdays. But my teachers said I needed to catch up. She was also pretty mad about me skipping class until I told her what happened. She told me if I ever got grief again about this "skipping incident," she would walk down to the school herself and give those folks a piece of her mind. That's the kind of person my mom is; after all, she was raised in Sherwood, a town of free thinkers and renegades: "Home of Robin Hood and his Merry Men." At least that is how she remembered it when she was young.

If the weather got nice, she now had to worry about Grandpa going out and wandering around. She would try and interest him in jigsaw puzzles, picture books, crossword puzzles, and even FOX News, but she said he was restless and had to be watched.

Robbery in the Sky

The next Friday, I came home reluctantly on the bus. Today was Homecoming. I would have liked to at least stay for the football game, but I would have to walk home in the dark. Besides I knew Mom needed me. Grandpa was out in the yard watching the sky. It was fall, and there were all sorts of geese circling in the still air. There were only a few puffy clouds drifting around and a cool breeze. Far above that, there were helicopters and small planes, and beyond that the trails of jet aircraft crisscrossing the sky. It was really an odd scene up there in the air. In the yard, Grandpa was turning around and around with his face up in the air. He looked like he was getting dizzy and started to stagger, so I ran up to the front porch and grabbed an old kitchen chair and dragged it out to the yard and got him to sit down.

We were distracted for a few minutes by a low-flying helicopter.

"I got it fig'gered out," exclaimed Grandpa.

"What figured out?" I asked.

"The economy–All fig'gered out. Those bigwig bank men are robbin' Peter to pay Paul," he said confidently.

"How can you tell?" I challenged. "Did you see that on FOX News?"

"No, I fig'gered it out right here. See those helicopters? Those planes? They are carrying money from one bank to another, a' bailin' each other out. Back and forth. Back and forth."

I thought that was probably not happening, but it made as much sense as anything else I had heard. "Grandpa you might just have something there," I teased.

"I know I do," pronounced Grandpa. "These planes and helicopters are special couriers. They just keep all that money up in the air! Hey! I just got an idea! Don't tell anyone about this. Why don't you and me—we are the only ones who know about this so, here's what we do: we rob those planes. We catch them in the air, and we rob those suckers of their money. Ha ha ha ha. "Why we could be like Frank and Jesse James. Like Robin Hood himself! 'Rob from the rich and give to the poor.' Well, of course, Lyle, we'd give your Mom some money too and—"

I was so fed up with this goofy plan by now. "How the heck would we do this? With pogo sticks?" I griped bitterly.

Indian Farming

On Saturday, the temperature soared for a few days, and we experienced what Grandpa called Indian Summer. We were walking up Old Highway 99, which was built just around the time of the Model A Ford. Now it was a subdivision of pretty nice houses, sort of like the one we used to live in called Woodhaven. Grandpa was leading the way, and Teddy and I were holding hands in back of him. At first we were just walking on a road, but soon there was an abrupt edge between country and suburb. The sun was beating down, and I felt like we were going to have to turn around and go back home soon.

"This was a big scrubland and grassland. That's what my old Granddad would say." Grandpa's voice trailed off as he waved his hands around. His bowlegs ambled several steps up the new sidewalk. On that little hill, we could see it was gutter to gutter houses as far as the eye could see. Their pointy roofs were mocking the pointy mountain barely visible in the background.

"What mountain is that, Grandpa?" I asked.

"Why, Mount Hood of course. One of the boy mountains that fought over the girl mountain," he said, winking at me.

Grandpa was either acting giddy or crazy. I could not tell which. Teddy thought he was funny and was laughing at him, which encouraged Grandpa even more. He raised his arms in the air and did a little circle. Teddy did one too. Then he flailed his arms in the air and started quacking like a duck. A passing car honked.

Grandpa's eyes gleamed in the sun. It was time for a story. "This land fed the Indians with tarweed an' camas an' deer an' wild birds. They farmed this brush patch by setting it on *fire!*" he shouted.

"What fire?" said a passing lady, walking her poodles. "No fire, ma'am," I said. "Say, Grandpa, I think it is time to go back to the house. It is getting too hot out here for Teddy."

"No, it's not," giggled Teddy.

"Historians call this fire farming pyro-agriculture!" said Grandpa. "They would burn the land, then harvest."

"That's interesting, Grandpa. Let's go," I said as I turned them around.

"Yeah, *fire*!" Grandpa shouted again; you could see he was amused. He looked at the development and took one more long look. "Yeah, fire." Then he turned slowly and walked away as if bushes were burning in his wake.

Up to Madge's

Well, so I missed Homecoming and even Halloween since we lived out on the edge of what used to be the country, and it was pouring down rain all night. Teddy and I would have been drowned just getting to the neighbor's house and back.

But the next experience I had sort of made up for no Halloween. It was Saturday, and my mom really wanted to get rid of Grandpa because some men were going to come in to check the roof and clean the chimney. I was going to take him on a long, long walk up Brookman Road, but as luck should happen, in the end, Grandpa took *me* on a long, long walk.

We meandered down the country road, and Grandpa would point out the name of a tree or tell me a story about some place. There was a strange-looking wooded area with no underbrush and very tall trees.

"In 1962, we had the Columbus Day Storm and many large fir trees blew over. They were down so far into the woods and the ground was too soft and swampy to take in a tractor or truck, pretty much all year. But the next winter, we had a big flood down there, and I floated a boat with a motor into the flooded swamp there. I was able to fish the logs out and tow them to the road and buck 'em up," Grandpa recalled.

Grandpa was going to show me the old Brookman house when a big old rusty truck came roaring around the corner. The truck slowed down as it reached us, and the driver rolled down the cab window. Then he braked right in the middle of the road.

"Old Man Lowe! Some kind of kid you got there!" sneered the guy.

Grandpa just sort of waved at the guy and nodded.

We were going to step away, but this guy was not done with us yet. "Hey you, yeah, you kid!"

"Yeah?" I said.

"You leave my kid alone. You hear me?" he yelled. "Uh, yeah. Okay. Who is your kid?" I asked.

"Wade. Don't you ever, ever touch him again! Do you hear?" The guy was leaning so far out of the truck, I thought he was going to fall out.

I started talking fast. "Okay. I've only seen him once when I was helping Benny, your nephew."

"You know what I mean, you rainbow boy, I will kill you!" With this, the guy roared off down the road, sending a cloud of black smoke up in back of him.

"Oh man, Lyle! Big man on campus, are we?" chuckled Grandpa. "You get into some fights?"

"No, Grandpa," I said as we continued to walk. "I just helped out this guy, Benny, who needed help taking care of his handicapped cousin. It was no big deal, and I don't know why he's so mad at me. I really don't get it."

"Well, let's go up to Madge's place," said Grandpa. "It's not too far and there are some pretty good things to look at up there."

We passed a big bend in the road with a high board fence, and then walked by a row of mailboxes. Then we turned down a dirt lane. There was a small field filled with llamas and alpacas. Beyond that, we saw a nice pond surrounded by walnut trees. There was a bunch of kids out there picking up nuts, so we wandered over there. Madge had out the troops: Billy and Millie and Joe, a second grader who rode my bus, and two other neighbor girls and their mom.

"Wow! You guys," said Madge as we approached. "Did you walk all the way up here?"

Grandpa chuckled. "We sure did, Madge. We came to pick walnuts! Put us to work."

Grandpa really just stood there, but it looked like fun so I got under a tree and put the nuts in a bucket. Most of the nuts were just lying around on the ground after they burst out of these green husks. Others were still in the husks, but they were cracked so you could see the nut in there.

"Don't pick the black gooey ones," Madge instructed. "Most of the gooeys are not good. We've had a pretty dry fall, so the husks have not all turned black."

In an hour, the work was all done. The neighbors went home, and we put away the nuts in the shed, which would be dried later, gathered the leaf rakes, and put them away, and washed out the buckets and our hands. Mine were a bit stained, but Madge's hands were really brown.

Going to "Crack in the Wall"

"Madge," said Grandpa, "let's take Lyle up to see 'Crack in the Wall.'"

"That sounds great," said Madge. "You kids go back to the house and watch cartoons. We are going to go on a long hike."

Then we were on our way up a well-worn path toward a horse paddock near a big barn, followed by a large field of sheep. The path entered a forest and almost disappeared. Madge led the way, picking up tree limbs as she walked and throwing them to the side. Old limbs from the past were the only markers for the path that I could see, but I soon learned there were more marks than that.

We came to a huge oak tree–the only one around. Way up, over our heads, there was a big slash in the bark.

"That mark points the way to 'Crack in the Wall.' We are halfway there," said Madge. We turned and kept on walking, but now we were going up a hill.

Then we came to a flat spot, and by the trail there was a large mutant-looking Douglas fir tree with a huge, thick limb that stuck out like an arm.

Madge stopped and pointed to the weird tree. "We've had an archeologist and his students come out here and they call these trees CMTs or culturally modified trees because some human has used these trees by marking them or stripping them. They think this tree was used to lay the dead to rest."

"They put a dead guy in a tree?" I asked.

"Yep," said Grandpa, "Indians never buried their dead in the ground around here. They were always put to rest in a tree or on a platform, or placed in boats."

We kept on going and finally reached a flat spot and came out of the woods. As we were walking I noticed that none of us had said much. Madge put her fingers to her lips as we crept out into a magical meadow. A doe and two fauns were on the other side of the creek. We watched them for a while until they walked away. We kept walking silently up the creek until the creek became sort of a swamp.

Barrump. Barrump. The sound echoed in the air.

We looked into the swamp, and there at the edge of it, we saw a brown puddle.

"Barrump!" said the slick puddle.

It was a big bullfrog sunning his back in the swamp.

Madge pointed up, and in the middle of the swamp was a big blue heron. I marveled at his stillness. How did he stand on one leg like that for so long without moving? We skirted the swamp a few yards more and came up to a big rock wall. The trail ended. Two large vertical slabs of gray rock held a trickle of water between its folds. Delicate ferns and moss surrounded the trickle of water.

"That is beautiful!" I exclaimed.

"And magical too," said Madge. "The Atfalati Indians camped here for many years on their way to catch the eels on the other side of this mountain at the Willamette River at the falls. The trail went somewhere from here over what the settlers called Wild Horse Mountain. My great-greatgrandfather and his family homesteaded some land on the other side of this mountain before Oregon became a state. That's why we know about this place."

Grandpa was running his hands up and down the rock wall. "One day a little Indian boy pulled some licorice fem off this wall and the mountain opened up to the other side. The little boy walked through, then came back and showed his family the way. They used the crack in the wall for a few years after that."

"Wow. That is a real Indian legend, Grandpa," I said.

"Yes, Lyle," said Madge. "The Brookman family heard that story from the Lightfoots who were real Atfalati Natives. My family was friends with them for a long time."

It was getting late in the day, so we turned back. Madge pulled me aside and said, "I have not seen your grandpa this active and alert for the longest time. I think you and your mother are really helping him."

I laughed. "Yeah, it just might be that we are getting used to him, but he doesn't seem so crazy anymore."

"So," Madge said, with a twinkle in her eyes, "are you from a tribe or a kingdom?"

"Uh, I don't know. My mom says she is from a tribe, but I really don't know what that means." I answered.

"Well, if you were from a kingdom, that means your allegiance is to a king, or perhaps in the 21st century, the federal government, or now since corporations have been ruled as 'people,' a corporation," said Madge.

"So what does a tribe stand for?" I said.

"Tribe stands for your family. Your ancestors and where you came from." Madge explained.

I made up my mind. "Well, then I am from a tribe. I can't see how any kingdoms are doing me any good."

Grandpa rejoined us again. "I'm going to drive you boys home," said Madge. "You've had a long day."

More Trouble at School

Mom was yelling at me from another room on Monday morning. "Lyle, don't forget to take the garbage out on your way to the bus, and don't forget to get more books for Grandpa."

"Yes, Mom." I hollered back. I'd get him some picture books of fall leaves and such. Maybe some books with pictures of waterfalls or horses. I grabbed two books from the table by the door to take back. He had one titled *Oregon Desert* that he glommed on to and would not part with. I have not seen that book out of his sight for a long time.

The bus was noticeably quiet when I got on today. Benny was already sitting with two boys so I sat by myself. I didn't catch up with him until we were in line for breakfast.

As soon as I saw him, I knew that Benny knew something by the way he was acting, so I asked straight out, "Hey, what is up with your uncle? He stopped me in the middle of Brookman Road and threatened to kill me."

Benny squirmed. "Uh, well, nothin'."

"What do you mean nothin'? I think your nothin' means somethin'," I pressed.

"Well, my uncle went to parent-teacher conferences, and the teacher told him that she heard from Ms. Betts that we were hugging in the changing room." Benny's eyes went to the ground.

"Oh I see how it is," I said. "Your uncle heard from an other person that we were doing something that she did not know anything about."

"Exactly," said Benny, beaming.

"First of all, that is hearsay from a second and even a third party. Did you try to tell your uncle or anyone else what was really going on?"

"I tried to," Benny said, clouds in his eyes were forming. "But the more I explained, the more my uncle, Mom, and Dad started screaming at me." Benny broke down and cried.

"This just really makes me mad." I hissed. "Oh yeah, it's okay for football players to hug after a touchdown or swat each other's behind to celebrate a good block, but it is not alright for a scared kid, intimidated by adults, to thank a friend for teaching him something he was being forced to do." I slammed my book on the table. "This school sucks!" The last thing I said was a bit too loud and some girls jumped up from the table nearby and hustled away.

I'm glad my mom didn't know that we had parent teacher conferences. I actually didn't know that myself. I was told by two of my teachers that the best I could hope for in their class was a D. It was really not a good day, and on top of that, things didn't get better after school. I took in my two library books, only to find out that the librarian was out sick for the day. In her place was this aide.

I took two new books up to the counter and laid them down for her to check out.

"You cannot check out these books," she said.

"Well, I turned in these," I said as I pointed to the return box with only my returns in it.

She scanned in the books and said, "How did you get so many books out in the first place? The limit is two. You still have out the *Oregon Desert.*"

"Oh yeah. I have that book at home and I told the librarian about it and she said I could keep it until Christmas."

"That is not the rules," she stated.

"Well, I'm getting them for my grandpa. We read them together and share them with my little brother."

The aide snorted. "Likely story. Now go away and put these books back on the shelf."

I just stood there and looked the lady in the eyes. "Look, I made a deal with the librarian and she understood. My poor old grandpa needs books to look at. I'm not making this up. Call her up and ask her," I begged.

"No way," she said firmly. "Now go put the books away."

I stood my ground. "No, that is your job," I said, as I scooped the books up and slid them to the floor. She stared at me like I was a monster. I was furious. "You are lazy and not very understanding," I blurted out. Then, I raced to the back room to get my rain slicker. With the bad weather, I asked the librarian if I could hang it back there for rainy nights when I had to walk home. The librarian walked to school too so we both had our stuff hung up there from time to time.

"Wait, wait," called the aide as she waddled after me.

"You are not allowed–"

I grabbed the coat and plowed on by her before she could even get in the backroom door.

I was supposed to be working in the library, but now I didn't want to stay there so I went to the English classroom to work. The door was locked, so I went to the biology room. The teacher helped me for a half an hour, and then she had to go, so then I went to the math room and got my work done there. Now that it is late fall I only have about forty-five minutes of daylight to walk home. I find it easier to walk the wrong way on 99W, and then climb over the fence and walk the back of the vineyard toward the house. It was "the dark time of year," as Grandpa called it. Not only was the daylight short, but the entire bowl of the sky, from horizon to horizon, was always gray, for days at a time even. Then, like a miracle, the gray would turn to puffy white clouds, open up to the blue, and the sun would shine. But I could see that there would be less and less of that as winter had just begun.

Worst News Ever

When I got to Pigeage, the place was lit up more than usual, and there was a big white car in the driveway with two little American flags on it. Could it be that Dad was home? I raced up to the porch. The porch light and hall lights were on, and when I made it to the living room, there were two guys in military dress, right down to their white gloves. I half expected to see my dad, but these guys were strangers and they were sitting on either side of Mom on the couch. She wasn't crying, but she looked like she was shocked. Grandpa looked very sad and old, and Teddy was sitting in the comer sobbing. The only person in the room that looked normal was Baby Mary, babbling by herself.

Mom jumped up from the couch. "Lyle! Where have you been? You should have been home a long time ago"

"I've been at school, Mom. Today's Tuesday. I'm supposed to be there late, doing my homework," I said. My mom blushed. "Oh, that's right. Sorry." She sunk back down on the couch. "Lyle, we have some very bad news... your father died last month."

"Last month?" I repeated.

Mom broke down and started crying. She had waited for me to come home before she started crying.

The military dude stood up. "So... folks, I am so sorry for your loss. It took us quite a few weeks to find you. Your husband died a hero, Mrs. Kent, and we will have a full military funeral in Washington, DC. What is your mailing address? You should be getting a large check in the mail to cover the costs of travel for you and your children. We also may have some transport help for you if you can get up north to Washington."

Mom didn't move, so I got out some paper and a pencil and wrote down our address. The other military dude got up and shook everyone's hands including Baby Mary. Grandpa moved from the couch to his chair and started wheezing like he was short of breath. I went over to him and rubbed and patted his back. The military dudes left, and we all just sat stunned in the living room the rest of the night.

The Nature of Things

I didn't go to school the next day or the day after that. The second day, I walked up to Crack in the Wall and just hung out in the rain in my yellow slicker. I didn't see Madge on the place going in or out on the trail, and I didn't go to the house to bother her.

On that night, there was a call from the school. Mom didn't answer it, I did. The counselor wanted my mom and I to come to the school for a meeting.

"I don't think this is a good time for that," I said. "We just found out that my dad died," I said.

"Really?" she said. "I'm so very sorry. Well, how about next week?"

"Well, maybe, if we don't go to Washington, DC." I really didn't care about school anyway. What have they done for me other than cause me grief?

The next week, there was no word or check in the mail. Mom made me go to school, so I grabbed my raincoat and books and went to the bus stop. Benny was sitting with the same two boys on the bus, and when I sat down, two senior boys moved over and one sat with me and the other one behind me.

In a high voice the first boy said, "Hey there, little 'rainbow boy' where have you been?"

"At home," I said flatly.

"Well, you better stay at home with your mommy, little rainbow boy, and leave Benny alone." This came from the second boy behind me, who grabbed some of my hair and yanked my head back.

"I will, I will leave Benny alone, but I've gotta go to school!" I said as I gritted my teeth. The pain was unbearable as the kid yanked out a piece of my hair. I screamed out in pain. "Agggh."

"What's goen' on back there?" yelled the bus driver.

"Nothin'," said the boys in unison.

Luckily, we pulled into the high school right then, and I shot off the bus as fast as I could. I ran straight to the library. Luckily, the librarian, Ms. Bricks, was there.

"Hi, Lyle! Long time no see, man." We gave each other a high five, and I asked if I could talk to her in the back room.

"Ms. Bricks, I'm having a hard time. We just found out a couple of days ago that my dad died a month ago." I started.

"Oh, I'm sorry to hear about that. How is your mom? Does she need anything?" I shook my head and Ms. Bricks continued. "What about your grandpa. How is he doing?" She sat me down in a chair.

"Mom is getting help from our neighbor and well, Grandpa is all right. You know he's really my great-grandpa," I said.

"Oh, I see," she said.

"My grades are bad in school, and I just can't understand most of the work. I've got kids giving me a hard time. They call me a rainbow boy. What the heck does that mean?"

Ms. Bricks hesitated a second. "It means they think you are gay."

"That's what I thought," I said. "But I'm not gay. People are making it up. One of the adult aides saw a younger kid hug me because I helped him and she told everyone: the teacher, the kid's parents, the kid's uncle, everyone on the school bus, a couple of bullies. This is nuts! Remind me, Ms. Bricks, to never, ever, do anything nice for anyone again."

Ms. Bricks smiled. "That is not in your nature, Lyle. You help your family and people because that is part of who you are. Do you belong to a tribe or a kingdom?"

I stood up. "I know what that means, Ms. Bricks. I hear that all the time."

"Well, then make that your commitment. You must be true to yourself," she said.

Ms. Bricks' lazy aide waddled up to the backroom door. "Ms. Bricks, you are wanted on the phone."

"I'll be right there. Thank you." But Ms. Bricks didn't leave to answer the phone right away. After the aide walked away, she went over to a shelf and took four books down and handed them to me. "These are all checked out, and they are all due before Christmas, as is the one you've still got. Enjoy them with your great-grandpa!" Then she let me out the back way into the hall.

Star High School

The last period of the day, the counselor came to get me out of class. She just laid out the whole pitiful record of my schooling: F in three subjects and a D in two. I was behind to begin with, didn't catch up, failed tests, and either skipped classes or was absent. All the absences were unexcused. What did I have to say for myself?

I decided that I should not say anything. You end up making excuses, and no one cares about your excuses. It means you are weak. I am not weak, and I have learned that I may care about the things that have happened, but again no one else does.

She decided to take me out of Sherwood High School and enroll me in Star High School. It was a statewide high school on the web made by another Oregon school district on the coast in Lincoln County.

"You get your own computer, and the courses are online. I'm sure you have a modem or wireless at home." She smiled.

"Well, no I don't. I think my mom uses the computers in the library now. She sold our laptop to buy clothes and stuff for the house," I matter-of-factly said.

The counselor turned red. "Oh, well, I suppose that you can use the wireless here at school and do your work in the library. Also you can use the laptop in the public library or the coffeehouse. Just get their Wi-Fi passwords."

She showed me the website and got the password to use at the high school from the tech people, and then told me to go to the library.

"Ms. Bricks, Ms. Bricks! You'll never guess! Look what I got!" I flashed the laptop at her. "I am going to an online school, so I can come here or go to the coffeehouse or public library and do my work!"

"Well, that will be good since you've got that long trip to Washington, DC," said Ms. Bricks.

"It's almost been two weeks, and we haven't got any word from the army," I said. "But this is so cool! I'm going to sit down right now and register for classes." I ended staying way, way after dark. Ms.

Bricks was waiting for her daughter to get out of play practice, so she gave me a ride home.

My New Computer

I burst in the door of the house. "Mom, Mom! I'm going to a new school! Look I got a new laptop!"

Mom whirled around from the sink. "Lyle, what on earth are you talking about? What's wrong with Sherwood High School?"

"I was way behind when I got here, and I just can't keep up. Everything is too hard. Not very many people like me, and they don't want me there either. So now I can come and go to the school or library or coffee shop or even a motel room when I travel, all I need is Internet, and then I can go to school! I don't have to take regular classes with kids and teachers!"

"Oh boy, what will they think of next?" said Grandpa dryly from the dining room table.

"Can we play games like Millie and Billie do?" asked Teddy.

"Uh, there's Tetris and Solitaire," I said.

"Well, remember, schoolwork comes first," said Mom.

First Assignment: Story of a Place

First Assignment: Story of a Place–that was all I had on my computer screen. It was my first English assignment, and I didn't know what to write. I had to have at least one hundred fifty words. I looked over at Grandpa. "What is a memorable place that you have been to, Grandpa?" Grandpa thought for a moment and started to laugh. "Well, Lyle, I've been to Boron. That's halfway between Moron and Boring. He he he. That's a play on words, Lyle. Boron, California is halfway between Mojave and Barstow. They mined boron to make laundry soap. You've heard of the twenty-mule teams? They used to be on TV ads during the show Death Valley Days. I drove truckloads of boron to the mills out of Boron. It is great western country."

"I've never heard of it, Grandpa," I said.

"Well, when you get on those interwebs, see if you can locate some information on it, like you did for me the other day at the library," he said winking.

A Big Black Cloud

The next day, I walked to the coffee shop in Old Town Sherwood, got the password, and a cup of horrible, strong coffee, and I was in seventh heaven all day on the computer–playing games, setting up a new email account, watching cartoons and YouTube, setting up a Facebook account and, oh, looking at the Tri-Stars High School website. I kept thinking about the writing assignment, but I really didn't know what to write. I just hated that. Here we are in high school, and we already have to know about places in the world we like, before we can write about them. Why doesn't Tri-Stars give us a ticket to Washington, DC, so we can really go somewhere and learn about stuff like US history and government?

I looked out the window. Some of the junior high kids were walking by, so it must have been about 3:00 p.m. A big black cloud was looming over Washington Hill and pushing its way toward the coffee shop. Suddenly the rain started dumping down on the street and sidewalk, and kids were dashing into the shop to get out of the downpour.

The two tough boys that yanked out my hair and threatened me on the bus walked into the cafe, all soaked, and they started to shake like dogs, splattering water all over. I tried to sink down in my chair and put my head near the computer screen. They were busy being the most important people there so I thought I was going to be okay, but one of them saw me as he turned around the room.

Naturally, he came sauntering right over to me.

"Well, it's rainbow boy at the coffee shop," he announced to everyone as he spun around the room. Most of the people looked at me, and then went about their business. The other boy, obviously distracted, came loping over.

"Why are you here?" the other boy said. I just ignored them and typed gibberish on the computer.

The place that I am going to tell the story about that that I am going to tell you about is very special and I think it is the best place. The Best place to be is the warm place with no rain and not tooo hot and it is perfect for getting around and. People would help each other the get along and help and maybe it could be happy and-

"*Did you hear me?*" yelled the first boy into my ear.

Without looking up and still typing I said, "Yes. Please leave me alone. I have a right–"

"*What* did you say, rainbow boy?" screamed the second boy.

The owner of the coffee shop came over. "Are we having a problem, boys? If so, I want you all to leave before I call the cops."

I looked at the owner. "I have been here all day, minding my own business, and I would rather stay here if these guys are going to go."

The second boy said, "He's a troublemaker, sir. I saw him harassing a girl and pulling out her hair the other day on the bus."

"*All* of you *out, now*," he spat.

The two boys stood there, so I thought if I went first, I could outrun them, so I yanked out my power cord, slammed the laptop down, swooped up my backpack and slicker, and made a dash for the door. My stuff was a jumble in my arms, and I managed to get out as a mom and her little kids were walking in. I decided I should run to the high school, and if I made it that far, hide in the library where at least there was one adult who would stick up for me. I glanced back and saw the boys running about a block behind. I jumped into the alley, and then swooped through a graveled parking lot. I saw one of the boys behind me. I looked forward–there was the other boy in front of me.

They grabbed my backpack and threw it in the mud, but I hung on to the laptop and the slicker. They dragged me into the alley, kicking and screaming for help. They grabbed the laptop and threw it in the mud and they started punching me. Somehow I still had the raincoat, so I pushed it up into a face and got it over the head. I started to swing the "raincoated" guy around, and as I did, the other boy kicked me in the ribs. Then they slammed me into the brick wall a couple of times each, and I melted down the side of the wall. That is all I remember.

I woke up to splashes of rain on my face. It was cool, and I thought it might be a good place to take a nap.

"Honey, are you all right?" asked this little old lady.

That really woke me up, and I started to move. My chest and legs felt like they had been slammed. I could see my yellow raincoat floating in a big puddle of water. "Could you get someone to help me up?" I whispered.

Two middle-aged guys from the nearby Rotary meeting came out to the alley. Slowly and very painfully, they got me standing up. I leaned up against the brick building. "My pack...my laptop." I cried. The men scoured the area and found the backpack in the parking lot. They found the power cord, but did not find the laptop.

"We've got to call the cops and get you to a hospital," said the older guy.

"No, I'm fine now. I'll report this when I get home," I said. I reached down and grabbed the dripping, muddy slicker and my bag. My body was in agony, but I tried not to wince. I started to walk away.

"No, wait," said the younger Rotary guy, "I'm taking you to your house right now. You really should report this. My car is just across the street."

Keeping Up Appearances

When I got home, I stashed my muddy things in back of my bedroom door and went straight to the bathroom to shower. I had lost my last chance to stay in school. What a stupid thing it was to show off that computer all over town. I just could not stay here any longer, but where could I go? It just reminded me of that stupid assignment–the story of a place. I used to be so happy. I used to live in a great place. Now what was there to really live for? I did not live there, and I was not happy. I washed my bruised shoulders and felt the keys around my neck. That was it! I would go back to Arizona and ask, no, demand to stay there. That would be the plan. I would get ready for a few days, and then I would leave. I would get what money I had and figure out a way to get out of Oregon.

That night, after dinner, my mom asked me how school was going. "It is really great." I lied. "I have new ideas for my writing assignment." I got some paper and a pencil and started writing.

"Why don't you do that on your computer, Lyle?" asked my mom.

"Because I am working on a rough draft first." Here is what I wrote:

The Story of a Place

People in Arizona have no idea that the state that they live in is the best place in America, and maybe the whole world, for all I know. First of all, you can go out and be warm and dry most of the time. That is not true in Oregon. Except for a few nice days, it is wet and cold.

Arizona was part of the Wild West in the old days. It was full of cowboys, Indians, miners, and people like gunfighters and bank robbers. It was exciting, and you could get what you needed to survive. I still think that there is a lot of opportunity in Arizona.

There are many kinds of people in Arizona. There are Mexicans, Black people, Indians, India Indians, Chinese, Japanese, Irish, plain old white people, and Texans. All of these people live together, and they all like each other and respect each other. If everyone gets along in one place, that has to be the best place to be.

This is the story of a place that I like. Arizona is where I came from, and I would really like to go back.

I counted every word and realized that I had over one hundred fifty. I only wished that I had my computer, so I could send it in.

Jacking the Goods

The next day, I had to look like I was busy, so I washed and dried my muddy bag and put the power cord in it. It is not a good idea to leave extra evidence around. Then I took out the rain slicker and washed it with a hose. I hung it up to drip dry, and I scoured around my room for things that I might be able to sell. I also asked my mom about the check for the Washington, DC, funeral. I thought I would hang in there and not leave if the family was going somewhere. She said that it still had not arrived.

Then I decided that I would go to the public library and send in my writing assignment. At least I would have tried to do my best. So I put on the clammy, wet raincoat and headed out to Old Town Sherwood, using the back way and staying off the main roads.

I got to the library and found a quiet computer—as far away as I could from the rest of the people. I wrote up the assignment and sent it in. I did a few exercises in math too. I was feeling good about trying to stay in school.

"Psst. Psst!"

I jumped out of my chair at the noise and looked around. My heart was pounding. I really didn't want to get caught by anyone, so I started to gather up my stuff.

"*Psssst, pssst!*" It was louder this time. I also caught a movement of hair over along one of the stacks of books. Then I saw a little head–it was Benny!

"Dude! What are you doing here?" I whispered as we dove under a large table at the far end of the room.

"I'm looking for you, man. I found a phone and a number to call your house at school when no one was looking. Your mom said you were at the library, so I walked over here instead of walking to the junior high. I heard about those guys jumping you," he said.

I turned red. "Oh, man. I am so mad about that, Benny, they 'jacked my Tri-Stars laptop.'"

"Yeah," beamed Benny. "I heard all about it, and I saw it this morning. They stashed it in a jammed locker-you know, one of those ones that don't lock? So I took Wade out into the hall first period, and *he* jacked it from them! He actually started laughing, and I had a hard time keeping him quiet." With that, Benny pulled the battered laptop from a grocery bag.

"Holy Crap!" I whispered. "I totally owe you!"

We gathered our stuff and headed out the back door, but we got stopped.

"Hey there, guys," said this big burly guy in a suit. "Shouldn't you be in school?"

"We are in school, sir." I flashed my Tri-Stars laptop out of the shopping bag, with its bright logo, only slightly scarred from the alley rocks.

"Okay. That's cool," he said. "You need your education if you're going to be a mayor like me."

"Oh yes, sir…Yes sir …," we said in unison as we quickly walked out the door.

The rest of the day we hung out at the picnic shelter at Snyder Park, far above the town and school.

Taking Off

If I was going to leave, it had to be right away and it had to be in the middle of the week so that I could get a good start without people suspecting anything. I looked up the train schedule and found a day when the train would go from Portland to the south. It would cost $140, and I had $100. I had a pretty good watch I could sell, but so far I could not find anyone that wanted to buy it. I could probably sell the laptop if I needed the money. I thought maybe I could make some money from bottles so I gathered up all I could. Madge saw what I was doing, and she asked me if I would take hers in too if she gave me a ride and I ran them through the machines while she shopped. I ended up with $37.43. Not enough, but at least it would get me down the road.

I realized that I was stalling around, but then I kept thinking that maybe I would stick around for Washington, DC. On Friday, three weeks after we got the bad news about Dad, we finally got a letter:

Dear Mrs. Kent,

Once again, our condolences on your husband's death. Enclosed is the travel check and bereavement pay for you and your children to attend services in Washington, DC. If it is possible for you to go to Seattle on Nov. 10, your family can take a ride on an army transport. The services are Nov. 14 at

Arlington National Cemetery. Please confirm your plans by telephone or email as soon as possible.

"Mom, tomorrow is November 14! We've got to get going!" I shouted.

Mom buried her head in her hands and sat down on the couch. "We missed the plane in Seattle. We will never make it." Then she started crying.

I grabbed the letter, and I felt like ripping it apart, but I didn't. I looked at the envelope. In the envelope was a check for ten thousand dollars!

"Crap, Mom! Forget about the funeral. It's too late. But look, Mom! This is a lot of money. We need a car! You could get a nice used car with this!" I carefully put the letter down on the coffee table. That was it. Mom would do okay with the kids and Grandpa, but I could not go on living here. I would leave next week and make a life for myself.

To the Southwest

On Monday, I had all my stuff ready. I took my backpack, a sport bag, and my laptop and left for Old Town Sherwood without anyone seeing me. I left a note on the table saying that I was going in to the coffee shop early to do my schoolwork. I hung out under the picnic shelter until the library opened, and I went in to email my homework.

It was about 11:00 a.m. and Benny came right in the front door of the library. He was on his way back to the middle school. I lowered myself to the table and got under it.

"Hi, Lyle," he said, ducking down under the table from the other side. "I'm thinking about Tri-Stars School too. I think the laptops are cool. How did you get it?"

"The counselor gave it to me, Benny," I said. "You could ask at the middle school, but I don't know if they have it or not."

"Well, it won't hurt to ask," beamed Benny.

"Excuse me, but would you boys like to join the rest of us up at the table?" asked a roving librarian. We both popped up at once. Benny came around the table.

"Look, Benny, I'm sorry that things got so crazy with your uncle and all," I said, since I was about to say goodbye forever.

"Me too," said Benny, looking down. "We aren't invited to Thanksgiving at my uncle's house this year. My dad and mom are really mad about it, and they yelled at me. It's all my fault."

I patted him on the back. "It's not your fault, Benny. Don't ever try to blame this on yourself. This is a secret, and I am only telling you. I am going away, Benny. After a while, everyone will forget what happened and everything will be back to normal."

"You are going to Washington, DC?" he asked.

"No, Benny. They already had the funeral. I'm going back to Arizona," I said.

Benny's face darkened. "You can't do that, Lyle. You are the only friend I have. I'm going with you. When are you going?"

"Right now," I said, hoping that would discourage him. "You really should not go with me."

"No, no! I want to go with you! I could go home and get packed. There's no one home today, and I have money."

"How much?" I asked.

"$250."

My heart sank. What other argument could I have? He might as well go with me, there was no reason why he shouldn't. "Really? $250? Well, okay."

As we were walking to Benny's house, Madge drove up and gave us a ride. I told her Benny got sick and had to go home, so she got us there in good time. I really rushed Benny. The only thing I made sure he had was the money. We quickly made it back to town with another ride and got on the bus. I was sweating it all the way because I was afraid we would miss the train in Portland. We got to Union Station with about ten minutes to spare.

"Where to?" asked the ticket man.

"Phoenix," I said.

He looked me and Benny over. "One way or round trip? 'Turkey Day Special'-you save on round trip."

Benny piped up. "Oh yeah, Lyle get a round-trip ticket, we would save—"

I hushed him and took him aside. "We aren't going back, Benny, we just want to get there. We aren't going to save any money." Louder, I said, "Remember, Benny, Dad said he would pay for our way back."

I looked at the ticket man. "Two one way tickets, sir."

"That will be $152 each." The man rung up the charge on the computer. You will have a layover in Sacramento, I think. We got out all our scrounged money out of a jar, wallet, and paper bag and counted the money. The ticket man just looked at us. "How old are you fellows, anyway?"

"I'm sixteen, almost seventeen, and my half-brother here is fourteen." Then I whispered at the ticket man. "Benny here has that midget disease." The ticket man saw the line was getting long so he printed the tickets and handed them to us, without looking at them.

The ticket man asked, "Do you have some sort of ID?" I showed the man my Oregon Trail Food Stamp card and a carefully prepared letter that I forged at Benny's house from my "mom" giving permission for us to go to our "dad's" place for Thanksgiving. There were lots of Thanksgiving travelers showing up, and it was a blessing that we had that smoke screen going on for us. We grabbed our tickets and dragged our bags and ourselves onto the train.

Back on the Road

You learn a lot about people when you are traveling with them. The first thing I learned about Benny was that he had never been outside the state, let alone outside the Portland-Metro area. The second thing I found out was that after an hour, he started having motion sickness. My brother has that too, so I knew of some tricks to use to keep Benny from getting sick. It was not a good idea for him to look out the windows from the side for a longtime. Nor was it good for him to focus in the train car, and then look out. Looking back and forth was really bad. In the snack car, which was upstairs, there was a window on top where you could look straight ahead, so we stayed up there for a good part of the time. There was snow in the mountain passes, and that was fun to look at. Then we went down into California and saw the dryer climate. This amazed Benny to no end. We had been sleeping in the seats the whole time, and I noticed that the conductor was looking at us and chatting it up with Benny a lot.

"Be careful what you say to that guy, Benny. We've got to stick to our story and not say anything extra," I warned.

The Science of Survival

The next day, a bunch of little kids discovered the observation window upstairs, so there was no long period of time for Benny to look out the window. We sat downstairs and played cards for a while. Finally, Benny threw down the cards. "I am really, really bored! We have done everything there is to do. I just want to jump off this train.

I reassured him. "It's okay to be bored, Benny. Try to get used to it. Let it come over you and just ride with it."

He hissed. "I *hate* it."

"You have to realize that being bored can be a natural thing while traveling. Some people sleep through it. Others find ways to cope with it."

Benny asked, "How do you do it?"

"I do a lot of thinking," I said. "Look I've learned quite a bit in the last few months about how to survive. There's a real science to it. This depression or recession, or bad economy, or whatever it is starting to make people crazy. Don't cave into it. Don't let it get to you. Don't let other people know how you really feel. Here's a couple of things I've learned for staying safe and sane in this world:

1. Always act like you know what you are doing–even if you don't.

2. Never give anyone too much information—ever.

3. Never make excuses, not that you don't have some, but people don't want to hear them, no matter how real they are.

4. Try and do your best to help other people. This can be a trading card. When you need help they can offer you something or at least cut you a deal.

5. When old people babble nonsense, listen because there is always truth in what they say, no matter how crazy. Remember they have a long history to draw from.

6. Finally, lying is okay for survival, as long as you aren't going to hurt someone.

"Wait," said Benny, "Jesus said lying is a sin!"

I just had to set Benny straight. "Well, yes that was in the Ten Commandments, long before Jesus, Benny, but there are ways you can lie. Like one is to not say anything. Or if someone is asking questions, you can always say, 'I don't know.' That's a good survival technique. We tell stories, and we don't call storytelling lying. What about a girl who is not pretty? When she asks if she is pretty, do we tell the truth and say she is ugly?"

"No, that would not be a nice thing to do," said Benny.

"So there you go, Benny," I said.

"My dad calls that tiptoeing around the topic," said Benny.

I grinned. "I bet Jesus had to do a lot of tap dancing to keep from getting the crap beat out of him."

The End of the Line

The train stopped in Sacramento, which really was a good sized city with skyscrapers and everything. People were moving to get off, but we just lounged around, waiting for the train to keep going.

The conductor was sweeping all the people from the cars, and he caught up with us in the upstairs snack car. "Okay, guys, it's time for you to get off the train."

"But we're not in Arizona yet," I said confidently.

"Yeah? Well, this is the end of the line for this train. Let me see your ticket."

Sure enough, the ticket was one-way from Portland, Oregon, to Sacramento, California, only. "What a rip!" I exclaimed. "What are we going to do?"

"I think you could get on the bus. The station is four blocks away. You've got two more days to get there for Thanksgiving," said the conductor.

So reluctantly, we got off the train and dragged our stuff four blocks to the bus station. (Little did we know that right after that, the conductor went into the train staff room. On the bulletin board, our school pictures were plastered in a poster that said, Oregon Runaways. He muttered, "That fig'gers.")

Bus Station

The bus station was full of people and gross. Most people looked like maybe they lived on the bus. One guy said he had been on a bus for twenty days going across the United States. We stood in line for almost an hour and found out when, where, and what bus to take.

"So ya want a ticket with that?" said the smiley ticket lady.

"Uh, I'm not sure. I'm asking for my mom, I'll get back to you," I said as I directed Benny out of the line.

"What are we doing, Lyle? Why didn't we get a ticket?" asked Benny.

"Because neither of us has $99," I spat. "That's why, Benny. We need almost $200. We need to sit down and think about this." We sat down in the hard plastic seats and soon a line bound for Salt Lake City formed right in front of us. There were large groups of people that looked like families in line. The kids were squirming in and out of the line, and when the line moved, the kids had to catch up, hustling and dragging their bags that they kept on the floor as the line moved along. There was lots of confusion at the bus door with all the groups of people and their offspring surging in and out of line. The bus driver was putting up with the confusion, but I could tell from his face that he knew this was going to be a long, long trip.

I turned to Benny. Despite the excitement and noise all around, he had fallen asleep. "Benny, Benny. I think I have a plan. We are going to go over to Door 17. That is where our bus is going to line up. We are going to start looking for families, but not too big of families, some medium-sized family. We'll pick one out, and I want you to sort of start chatting with one of the kids. We want to get in line right in back of them, and at the last minute, as the mom or dad are showing their tickets, you will sort of push ahead, maybe under or around the parent and see if you can get on the bus. I'll follow you. I want you to rush into the bus, not take your time, but at the same time you have to do it smooth, like you belong to the parent and maybe you are younger than you really are, you understand."

Benny's eyes gleamed. "Okay, Lyle! It'll be like a movie and we are Number 7!" (That is what Benny always called 007.)

"Right, Benny, just follow my lead, no matter what happens," I said confidently.

The whole plan came at the right time as we watched for our prey. We were alert to the people, and we actually evaluated them on their preoccupation with their children. The less the better, we figured. The kids had to be just squirrelly enough too. While Benny was chatting it up with a girl, I also noticed that there were some cops roaming around the bus station with a piece of paper in their hands, looking at the paper and all the people. I probably would not have even noticed this if we had not been casing the station as well. I moved our stuff near a flakey family of five-one mom and four kids. I struck up a conversation with the mom. She laughed and patted me on the back when I told her one of Grandpa's jokes, and I noticed that one of the cops walked the other way.

Soon the line formed, and we fell in with the flakey family. It was a dream come true, because one of the kids, a little girl, really needed some help and so I told the mom that I would help watch the three-year-old. She had a baby in her arms that was teething and screaming. The older girl was the mom's too, but Benny and the girl were so caught up in each other that they were not paying attention to anything. The other two were very active boys who always seemed to be playing chase with each other. We got up to the bus door, and the mom shoved the handful of tickets at the bus driver. The baby screamed, the little girl peed her pants right there on the bus driver's shoe, and one of the little boys left his bag on the ground and the whole line had to pass the bag to the front of the line. Benny and the girl smiled and giggled at each other as they got on the bus. Every seat on the bus was taken before we left. (Especially since there were two more passengers on the bus than there were supposed to be.) I was a bit worried about this, so I took my jacket off and put it on my lap and let the wet little girl sit with me. I noticed that Benny and the girl who was flirting with him were sharing the same seat next to the window, because they were so small, skinny, and oblivious to everything. I was in the middle seat, but outside the bus, I could see the two cops. "Benny, don't look outside." I warned. He immediately did and both he and the girl were waving out the window. "Benny, for the love of God, stop!" I hissed.

Back on the Road

When we got to Barstow, the flakey family got off the bus. *What a God-forsaken place to have Thanksgiving,* I thought. I grabbed Benny by the collar and gathered all our stuff. When the bus driver left the bus, we quickly moved to the very back of the bus.

There were still a few other people continuing on, so I was hoping that we could still mix in. "Duck down and stay down!" I hissed at Benny as we slowly bent our bodies to the seats. We stayed that way for quite some time. The bus was quiet. New people filed into the bus, but luckily it was not full.

Then the driver boarded the bus with a piece of paper in his hand. I was sure the driver was going to spot us. Soon the bus motor roared back on, and we were moving again.

Benny was asleep on the seat, and I let him stay that way. Soon I peeked out from between the two seats to see what was going on. The bus driver was pretty busy driving, and everything looked pretty calm. I could see out the sliver of a window that we would be in Needles soon, which meant we would cross the state line into Arizona.

007 in Phoenix

I woke up with a thump. My head banged the window. We had been on the bus for hours.

Benny started shaking me. "I think we are in Arizona, Lyle! Man it is hot and dry!"

Everyone was hustling to get their stuff off of the bus. We just watched them and stayed put. I could see that there was a small sign that said something about the Phoenix House restaurant, so I knew we were in the right place. I was afraid that the bus driver would be at the door, letting people off the bus. Then, I saw the driver messing around with the luggage hold, so I knew there was a better chance of getting off the bus.

"Have you got all your stuff, Benny? Because when we get to the door, you must be prepared to get away from the bus fast, don't go into the station, just go down the sidewalk, and maybe even run. Got it?"

Benny's eyes gleamed, "Got it Number 7!"

We got to the door with me leading the way. The door was closed, and I tried to quietly pry the door open. Benny found some sort of door lever, and I practically fell out of the bus. We both got on the ground and were slowly leaving when I heard: "Hey you kids, stop right there!" It was the bus driver.

Benny stopped and I grabbed his arm, and we ran out to the street and a sidewalk. I heard a whistle and someone running, but I didn't look back. There was a big department store ahead of us, and I knew that there was a couple of doors in that store that went out into the next street. We swept through there and kept on running until we got to a bus stop. There was a bus there, and we just got on it in time.

"Your fare, please," said the driver.

We scrounged every penny we had and threw it all in the meter. It was probably not enough, but the lady didn't say anything. That was when I realized that we were going in the opposite direction from where we wanted to go.

Back to the Cul-de-sac

"Boys, this is the end of the line" the lady bus driver. "Thanks," I said. "But could you help us? I need to get to bus 86."

She laughed. "You guys must have been traveling the wrong way. Here are some transfers. Take 16 and get off on Main Street, and you should connect to bus 86."

So we got back on the next bus and backtracked to the other side of town and my old neighborhood. I don't know what I planned to do when I got there, but at least it was somewhere familiar. I thought that we could maybe stay with Kate or go back and stay at my aunt's. So when we got off the bus, we walked to Kate's house first. The first thing I noticed was that there were no cars there. Not even one of the brother's hot broken-down cars. Neither of the two family cars was there. The place looked empty. And there was a sign at the corner of the yard, Phoenix Reality and a sign tacked on to it that said, Foreclosure. Kate was gone.

"Is that your house?" asked Benny.

"No, it was my friend Kate's house." I just stood there in shock. How could this happen to Kate's family?

We walked down the main road and saw a few more houses for sale. Then we came to my cul-de-sac. There it was, right in the middle of the street bubble-my house.

Benny was babbling. "Wow, Lyle, this was your house? You must'a been rich! Look at this place! It's huge!"

I was silent as we walked around it. There was a "for sale sign" in the front, and there was a huge blue padlock on the front door. There was another padlock on the back door too. There was a side door that was a possibility that they may have missed. It was sort of a maze because you go through a gate, then zig and zag to the garbage cans and a door comes out from the kitchen. I knew that area well I since I took all our garbage. In back of that is another gate that goes to the backyard. There were two more padlocks on the fence gates, so we rolled a garbage can over, climbed on top of it, and went over the fence. The side door had no padlock, so I took the key off my neck and sure enough, the key worked and we were in!

The house was very empty as we walked through it, Benny was still babbling about the place. We picked out rooms to sleep in. I chose my old room but once we did all that and got settled, there was nothing else to do. No electricity and of course no TV or radio. There was also no water or gas.

"It's going to get dark soon, Benny, so let's see what we can find in the kitchen. We found a few funky candles, a matchbook, cans of spaghetti, refried beans, green beans, and chili, some old forks and a heavy knife. Out in the garage there was a hammer, another book of matches, and a gallon of bottled water.

"Well, Benny," I said "At least we can hang out here for a couple of days." We took the hammer and pounded the knife into the can of chili and ate it cold. It was the first food we had eaten in a day and a half.

When we finished, Benny said, "Well, do you think today is Thanksgiving or tomorrow?"

We had no way of knowing. My watch only told the time, and there was nothing in the house to tell us. So we decided that Thanksgiving would officially be tomorrow. We didn't sleep very well that night. It was cold and all we had were our clothes to sleep in.

Thanksgiving Day

It was a rude awakening in the morning when we heard someone pounding on the front door.

I looked out the window and saw two really young adults out there. They saw me.

"Hey, you, you in there, come on out here!" yelled the guy.

"Just a minute," I said. "I've gotta come around the back." I got an old chair and climbed over the fence. Then I walked to the front yard. "Hi!" I said to the people.

"Hi," said the man. "Can you show us the house?"

"No, not really, I mean, my mom is about to get the house back, so it will be off the market soon," I said.

"Oh, too bad," said the lady. "I would love to raise my family here." Then I saw that she was pregnant.

"Well, so would my mom," I said grumpily as I turned and walked away from them.

"Who was it?" asked Benny, as I returned. "Someone wanted to buy the house," I said.

"Oh, man, you should have sold it to them. We would have enough money to get a smaller one and have money for food," he said, disappointed.

"It's not that easy, Benny. You've got to have papers and banks and real estate agents and all that to buy a house. People don't just dump a pile of money on your doorstep."

"That's too bad," said Benny.

We had a great Thanksgiving. First of all, we found some old Candy Land and Hungry Hippo games that my mom left behind in Teddy's room. Then we had our can of spaghetti and green beans. Then we digested our food by reading comics all afternoon.

Buddy, Can You Spare a Quarter?

The next morning, I heard a familiar sound: our neighbor warming up his car to go to work, followed by the other neighbor's truck. It sounded like a Monday, and everyone was going to work. Unless Benny was holding out on me, we had exactly seventy-five cents. There was nothing more to eat except the refried beans, and we even needed water. Benny was sound asleep so I wrote him a note:

Benny:

I'm going into town to get some food and water. Hang out in my room and keep watch at the window. If the real estate person comes, grab all our stuff and lock yourself in the upstairs bathroom. I think my mom lost the key to that bathroom. By the time they figure that out, they will have to fix the door, and we can be out of there so prepare for the worst. Otherwise, be a good Number 7 and read the books and comics in my bag.

Lyle

I walked down to the bus stop, and I saw several people being panhandled by a bum. I liked his line. "Oh heck, I need one more quarter to get on the bus. Does anyone have a spare quarter?"

I walked up the street to the next stop and tried that out. I got two quarters; one for the bus and one for a cup of coffee. (Of course that guy must have been joking!) Then I walked to another bus stop. This time, all I really did need was a quarter and that is what I got. The bus ticket was exactly $1.50. I got a transfer and got off at the library. I hung out until they were open, got the Wi-Fi password, and got on my computer. I did a couple of history lessons on Star School and took a test. Then I looked at my English page. I got an A on my "Story of Place" assignment! I was so excited! The next assignment was to take the place I just wrote about and write a fictional scene. I thought that was sort of cool to build on an assignment like that. I watched the time because I only had my transfer for an hour and a half. So I closed my computer and decided that I should raise some more money for food.

Already outside, there was a man selling newspapers. I asked him about the gig, and he gave me a card to get papers. He gave me eight papers and told me that if I moved five blocks down the street I could sell the papers for fifty cents. So I did that. It was not too easy until I found a doctor's office to stand in front of. I made enough money for two burgers and two bottled waters. Then I had to get on the bus. I barely made it.

Now that I was in walking distance, I decided to sell my last two papers for bus money tomorrow. I was so hungry that I ate my burger before I got back. It was getting to be around 4:30 p.m. when I got back to the cul-de- sac. As I rounded the comer, my hair stood up straight on end! There was a huge group of people in front of my house! The cops were there, the fire department, an ambulance, neighbors, and other people standing with the young adults I met yesterday.

"Lyle!" said a familiar voice that made me jump. It was my neighbor next door. "I haven't seen you in a long time. What are you doing here?"

I totally acted like I still lived in the neighborhood. "Well, I heard all the noise and realized it was here at my old house. What's going on?"

"It seems like there have been two vagrants living in your house. I don't know how people like that manage to get into a place like this. They've got it locked up like Fort Knox!" he explained.

"I don't know either," I said as I felt the keys around my neck under my shirt.

My neighbor didn't notice because his attention was on a huge bunch of yelling coming from the front door. "Oh, this should be good." He chuckled.

Then I saw what was going on and my heart broke. There was Benny in handcuffs being lead out by two cops. He was just hysterical. Without thinking I rushed up to them, but another cop blocked me and asked what I was doing.

"I want to help my friend!" I yelled.

"So you must be the other vagrant. You have a right to remain silent."

Jail

I don't know where Benny went; he didn't get put in jail, though. After all, he was only thirteen. I, on the other hand, was put in a jail cell. So what's it like being in a jail cell? One word: *boring*. But I've been training for boring times for quite a long time now what with train and bus travel, living in the country, and without regular computer or Internet entertainment. All you can do is sit and stand. I started doing some exercises from gym class too. I did get three meals a day and that was really good. I even took a shower. Everything I owned right down to my underwear was under custody. Just as I was getting used to the routine, something new happened.

Interrogation Room

So the cop parks me in the interrogation room–just like the ones I've seen on TV. What a cliché, if I ever saw one.

"Hi, uh"–the interrogator looks at his file–"Lyle. So, what do you have to say for yourself?"

"My name is Lyle Kent and I go to Tri-Stars School." I figured that would shut him up.

"Okay, that is what it says right here." He flicked his fingers at the file. "It also says you are a runaway from Oregon."

"You could call it that, but I could also call it "moving to Oregon" or "traveling from Oregon" or even "visiting from Oregon." I said matter-of-factly.

"So you're a wise guy, huh, Lyle?" he said standing up.

Without emotion, I said matter-of-factly, "No, sir, I am not a wise guy. I had to leave Oregon because of threats on my life–I have witnesses–I was being harassed, I got beat up, and my laptop was stolen."

"Really?" I could tell he was not buying my story. "But somehow you got your laptop back."

"Yes, I did, thanks to my friend and his cousin," I said. (I figured they weren't going to put Benny and Wade in jail. If they did, that was going to be the cops' problem.)

The interrogator strolled around. "So, you crossed two state lines with an unwilling minor and became a vagrant."

"Well, Benny, was not unwilling, sir, his family didn't want him around anymore, but yes, we became vagrants. Is being homeless against the law?"

He ignored my question and checked his file. "It says that, you will turn fifteen next week. If you would have waited a little longer, you would be going to the State Pen."

"I don't think I could have waited any longer, sir," I said. The interrogator put his hands on the table and stared at me. "Do you think that you made a wise choice?"

"Yes, I do, sir. I am safer here than I was in Oregon," I said.

There was silence. I was calm and steady. I did not move a muscle.

Mr. Interrogator was thinking. Finally, he said, "Okay. Go back to your cell, and I want you to think about what you have done."

Not Thinking About the Past

I did not think about what I had done. I did the right thing and as far as I was concerned, I was ready to move on. I asked if I could have my Tri-Stars computer to do schoolwork, and they said that I could use it one hour a day since it was used for education. That was really big of them. It was the first time I ever got excited about doing schoolwork.

Assignment Two:
Descriptive Story of a Place
Horse Line in the Desert
by Lyle Kent

Some people claim that the desert is all the same–that it is hot, monotonous, and really boring. But I have seen things around every turn, through every wash, across every mountain. Things that would make your head swim. The most amazing thing I have ever seen was on an old horse trail.

I was minding my own business, alone on the trail, looking for cactus flowers, and jackrabbits when I heard a muffled sound in back of me. I slowly turned to see a horse and rider appear on a rise. "Wheels yield to feet and both yield to hooves." It is custom in the desert to give horse riders the right of way, so I found a place off the trail to let the rider by. As I turned around at the stopping point, I saw that it was not one horse but a horse line; nine riders, all together moving at an even pace. Watching them like that as they came around a bend reminded me of a well-oiled locomotive. The horses' bodies and legs were churning like the drivers and wheels of the train, kicking up dust on the trail.

As the line drew near, I saw that the first man looked like a cowboy with a big, white hat and a bright red checkered shirt. Next was a Mexican from Mexico wrapped in a striped serape and a broad-brimmed, golden-trimmed sombrero. Next in the line was a dark faced Native American woman with a red shawl and large square leather purse. After that there was a young girl with yellow pigtails and a cowboy hat, followed by a dusty-looking man on a mule, not a horse, with a caved in stained felt hat.

It seemed like everything was moving in slow motion. The sun was bearing down on me like a furnace. I thought I'd say, "Hi! Where are you going?" But I was almost afraid to do that. They were very focused on their riding and the trail ahead. I was afraid I would spook the horses and maybe even the riders themselves. None of them greeted me even though I was an arm's length away. The saddle leather creaked and groaned around the beasts, and there was the crunch, crunch, crunch of the horses' hooves on the gravel.

The next rider was a man followed by a lady. They were both dressed like they had just been in a Wild West movie. The man, in a black hat, looked like a saloon gambler with a bulletproof red silk vest. He kept looking back to his lady who was actually riding sidesaddle in a long purple velvet dress. "Hi," I said to the lady who was looking my way. She looked right through me, like I was just another cactus on the trail. I felt like a ghost. Following the couple was a young black guy wearing a blue civil war hat and another older lady dressed in denim riding gear. The last guy was a cowboy with his black hat bouncing down his back.

What an odd group of people, completely silent and unaware that someone was watching them. I thought it was strange because when you are out in the middle of nowhere, you expect to exchange some words. It was as if the horse line represented a cross section of Arizona, working their way across the desert. The trail led down into a wash and came up the other side over another rise. I expected to see the horse line to come up within sight. But I did not see it. I kept looking, looking, looking for them ahead, scanning the horizon, but never caught another glimpse of them. All day I looked for hoofprints and horse scat and found nothing. How did they ditch me so fast? I scanned the horizon and looked for dust, but found no trace of the horse line.

I got back to the trail head, just as the golden sun was setting. "Did you see the horse line out there?" I asked a hiker who came off the trail ahead of me.

He shook his head. "Horse line? No I didn't see any horses all day."

"There were nine of them." I shared.

He chuckled, "Nine of them, you say?"

"Yes," I said, "they looked pretty strange. I don't think they even saw me."

"Probably not," said the hiker. "You're pretty lucky. You saw 'The Ghost Line of Arizona Flat.' Not many people have seen that out here. Most people only see a boring old dry desert."

Incoming

Clank, clank, cree. The jail cell door protested as it opened. It was either late at night or very early in the morning.

The night guard spoke in hushed tones. "Get on in there guys, there's a whole bunk bed there for ya." Flashlights were being aimed around. "There's another kid in the other bunk, and so help me, if you wake him up, I'm gonna make your stay in this hotel a little longer. This emergency light over here is only gonna be on for ten minutes, and then it will automatically go off. Got it?"

"Uh, yeah, yeah," said one of the guys.

The door protested again as the jailer locked it. You could hear him walk down the hall.

The guys—there must have been two—started giggling. "That was so funny, he he he, when that cop went down on his butt!"

"Yeah," whispered the other guy. Two scores, man, a tagging and a heist, right before breakfast!" They were giggling like girls.

Their voices got louder and louder, and normally I would have jumped up and told them to be quiet, but I didn't want to cause any ill will in case I was stuck with them for too long. The light went out, but they kept talking as if they needed to be louder if they couldn't see each other.

Suddenly, all the lights were on and the night jailer came back down the hall. I sat bolt upright in bed.

"See there," said the jailer. "You woke the kid up. I'm writing you up for insubordination, and we'll squeeze a couple more days outta you guys. Wanna go for a few weeks? We could put you in County."

The guys shook their heads and looked a little scared. Then, all the lights were on until 7:00 a.m. the next day.

The Bailout

At 8:00 a.m., we got our breakfast, which was oatmeal. The other inmates took one look at it and put it back down. I ate mine hungrily.

"What are you in for, kid?" asked one of the guys.

I looked at them. They were probably the same age as me, and yet I was the "kid."

"Attempted murder," I said.

That actually shut them up and I was glad. I was now waiting until lunch. After lunch, I got to have my computer for school. I was studying the concrete wall in my cell and imagining the men building it when I heard the guard come up the hall.

"Kent, you have a visitor." He unlocked my cage and took me down to the visitor room. There was my Aunt Peggy.

"Lyle, you owe me big time. I had to take a day off of work to come down and bail you out."

"I'm sorry, Aunt Peggy. I really didn't mean to get you mixed up in all of this. I will get a job and pay you back," I said.

"Well, you won't be just paying me back, you'll be paying your great-grandpa back. You have caused a world of hurt and tears and anguish, young man. Everyone in Oregon needs you, Lyle, you just can't up and run off like that," she said in a huff.

The guard on my side of the visitor's room handed me an envelope. It had already been opened.

"Read that, Lyle," said Aunt Peggy. "It's from your great grandpa."

The letter was written in ink and was a real hen scratch.

It took a few minutes to read the whole thing.

Dear Lyle,

I was very sad when you left us and so were your mom and Teddy. We feel like there is a hole in our life. Then, we heard that they had you in jail and that you needed to be bailed out. I always keep a bail fund in the bank for when I or someone else gets stuck by the law, but mercy, boy, what did you do? Rob a bank? $550 is a heck of a lot of money! Anyways I'm proud of you, boy, and I hope after you get out of the slam, you will come back home to Oregon.

Yours, Great-grandpa Lowe

I just didn't know what to say. My aunt said that I was going to get out today, as soon as they processed the money. "You can stay with me on the couch for three days, but after that, I am putting you on a bus. I've got a cousin coming in from Texas, and he has two job interviews lined up. I expect you to go home and not pull any more tricks, because if you do, no one will bail you out next time."

I was still not sure what to do. I got out of jail and went home with my aunt. I needed to think about things.

Epilogue:

A Voice in the Air

He sat on the broken rubble of rock and stared out into the setting sun. There was something in the sky, or maybe it was something in the air that was trying to communicate with him. You could see forever out here in the desert. That butte over there looked maybe a mile away, but on the map it was twenty miles. Even the stillness in the air was talking to him, and Lyle felt like this spot was where he wanted to stay forever. Blue sky was turning to purple and pink in every direction.

There was a gust of wind, and then another. The wind was humming and the dark purple mountains were calling:

Learn to give and not to want,
For the mountains are not giving,
Nor do they need.
They stand stoically,
Raising their arms unto the sky.
Mother Earth and Father Sky;
They are always there for us,
Weak children, that we are, by and by.
He stood up and looked all around, trying to memorize this place. He knew what he was going to do.
The End

Afterword

The story that you have just read is fiction, which of course means that it was made up. However, as with all good stories there is a kernel of truth to it or it would not be a good story. All of the people in this story have made-up names to protect the innocent as well as the guilty.

I started gathering the idea for this story in 2008. Other newspaper articles and conversations have entered this story. Off and on from 2008 to 2012, bits and pieces of ideas associated with this story were collected in my writing journals. I decided that I would write out this story for the National Novel Writing Month, and although it does not meet their goal of fifty thousand words, the story is here and complete. I would like to thank the NaNoWriMo people for their contribution to the success of this story.

June Reynolds